Asleep at the Keyboard

By Frank Adkins

Higher Ground Books & Media
Springfield, Ohio.
http://highergroundbooksandmedia.com

Printed in the United States of America 2019

Introduction

Asleep at the Keyboard is an eclectic mix of original short stories. Topics include thoughts from a habitual speeder, a middle schooler's redemption, love that endures following death, and a stepfather's greatest gift. In selecting these stories, it was my goal to include something for everybody. While it is my wish for at least one of these tales to resonate with you, I hope you enjoy them all. Thank you.

-Frank

Contents

Finding Peace on a Spring Evening

Leaning over the edge I peer downward, expecting to find total darkness. *My God, I can see the water. I didn't think I'd be able to be able to see the water!* I squeeze my eyes shut and grip the cold, rough concrete railing. My head swirls with vertigo and my stomach twitches. Tipping my head upward I try to focus on the sounds of the traffic behind me, but all I can picture are the white caps glistening like diamonds against the sea of black so far below. Cars and trucks rumble past. I can feel the vibrations through the retaining wall and pavement on which I stand. I hadn't expected this. It all seems too visceral, too real! *Breathe!* I tell myself. But after several deep breaths my hands still tremble, and my pulse still hammers in my temples.

I squat and press my back against the concrete wall. More deep breaths. I try once more to shift my thoughts. I envision the passersby. Who are they? What do they think about the Geo parked in the right lane, emergency flashers blinking, apparently broken down? And what do they think of the figure propped against the railing just within the periphery of their headlights?

At once I catch a chill. Only then do I realize just how windy it is up high above the Delaware River. Earlier in the day there had been a refreshing breeze stirring the air—air that was unseasonably warm for early April in Delaware. And it was on the deck of Augie's Tavern, overlooking the cool, inviting ripples of this very river, that Jennifer and I had sat sipping our Coronas. Amidst those gentle puffs of springtime air, she had leveled with me about the reason for her strange behavior of late. Suddenly she rose and turned away, and just as suddenly, I was alone.

I snap from my reverie as a bug crawls down my cheek. I swat at it, only to find that it isn't a bug at all, but a tear. A bus slows, then merges with traffic in the next lane as it passes my car. By the dim light inside I spot a teenage girl sitting near the back. She makes eye contact with me briefly, then looks away. For a moment I am sure it is Jennifer, only years earlier.

"You idiot," I mutter to myself, but then the stream of tears begins, and I weep. I weep for the happiness I've lost, for the uncertainty ahead, and for the high tide of despair that swallows me up like the Delaware River swollen from the springtime rains. I weep for the ache in my heart and for the emptiness, the *hollowness* that consumes me. But mostly, I weep for my lack of courage to face my lonely plight, and for my loss of desire to press on. How can a man as hollow as I ever be whole again? Finally, I weep because I know my own bus had reached the terminal after making its last run. 29 years of sorrow upon sorrow has brought me to this moment. I should be used to it by now, but each time it hits me as if for the first time.

Get a hold of yourself! my inner voice hisses. Once more I stand and peer over the railing at the whitecaps below. *Jesus, it's a long way down.* I never expected to be able to see the water at night, full moon notwithstanding. But from high up in the darkness the water of the Delaware doesn't appear cool and inviting now. It looks murky, mysterious, and uncaring. Patient, yet eager to claim me as its own.

This is all wrong. It's not supposed to be this way, the voice inside me says. I shake my head. No time for that now. I am on a mission. Regardless how I'd imagined things up here, this is how they are. I have to see my mission through. I'm not turning back. I can't let myself turn back. If I allow myself that option, in this weak moment it's the one I'd surely choose. No, my mind is made up. I am here

for a reason, and I have to act quickly. Help will arrive shortly.

But then, is there *really* any help? Could there be? Does it matter?

I think not. Either way, the authorities will soon arrive, uncaring of

my desire for them to stay away and determined to foil my mission.

Suddenly the irony of my situation hits me. I am so terrified at the

thought of being without Jennifer—of being without *anybody,* that

I've allowed myself to fall into the grip of my other phobia—

heights. On a different day, and if not for the gravity of my plight, I

might have found humor in it. What the hell was I thinking?

I blink away the tears. Just then a strong gust of wind hits me from

behind. Goose pimples spread across my forearms and I shudder

with chill. Instinctively I turn toward my car for my jacket, but then

I see the flashing blue and red lights approaching in the distance.

The authorities are indeed on their way.

I look back toward the water and am overcome with what feels like

vertigo, but then I realize it's something more. It's as if, in my head,

I've stepped back from my eyes and at once I've become nothing

more than a spectator, watching through the eyes of another as he

carries out my mission. I merely observe. I find comfort in

relinquishing control. I close my eyes and relax, waiting to find out how this movie ends.

The slam of a car door behind me jolts me from my thoughts. *Ignore the flashing lights,* I tell myself. But now I am warm. My goose pimples have abated, and the wind is as refreshing as it was earlier in the day. I think of Jennifer. It occurs to me that if I am to preserve the love, I have for her, to freeze it in time right here and in this moment, there is but one way. With that realization comes relief. I smile and breathe deeply of the cool air. Yes, I know how to make my love last for eternity and ensure that I will never be alone again. I am ready. I close my eyes, hold my breath, and reach for the whitecaps below.

Finding Fatherhood

I hurried home from work, eager to be with my new family. Kristy and I had been married for less than a month, but already Friday night had been established as family pizza night. My stepson Nick was fifteen, and he worked at a home improvement store after school. His sister Katie was twelve.

Kristy met me on the porch. "Asshole is moving to Florida. He's leaving tonight," she said, speaking of her ex-husband. "He went to Nick's work this afternoon to tell him. Can you believe that bastard didn't bother to come by and see Katie?"

Having witnessed his succession of broken promises and the false hopes he had instilled in the kids over the last two years, nothing he did—or didn't do—surprised me anymore. "Did he call her at least?"

"Oh yeah, he called her, but not until much later. By then, Nick had already come home and told her."

"How are they taking it?" I asked.

"Nick seems to be taking it okay, but Katie is devastated."

Nick was the strong, silent type, much like his mother. He processed things internally. Katie was just the opposite. Her face hid nothing, and expressions of her thoughts and feelings tumbled from her mouth unchecked.

I was a second-time husband, but a first-time father, fumbling to find my place within their family. Although I had no children of my own, I couldn't imagine loving any kids more than I loved these two. Still, as a new parent I felt lost much of the time. Kristy and I agreed that I had to be a role model, not a friend. In setting guidelines and enforcing our rules I had to be firm, yet not too forceful. Secretly, I feared that if I got it wrong the whole family dynamic would collapse around us. *How does one find that balance?* I wondered. Already I had developed a pattern of handling each new situation the best I could, then second-guessing myself to the brink of madness afterward.

The door opened and Nick appeared. "Mom, are you ready?"

She nodded. "I'm taking him to Dillon's house."

"How are you doing?" I asked Nick.

"Okay. Dad's moving to Florida."

"Yeah, I heard," I said. "You alright with that?"

"Why wouldn't I be? He says it'll be good for him." But the flash of pain in his face said otherwise. "Come on Mom."

Kristy kissed me. "I'll be back."

Prior to our wedding, Kristy and the kids had moved from their home in Dover, Delaware to my house in Smyrna. Dillon lived in Milford, easily an hour away in Friday night beach traffic. Nick and Dillon were best friends, and I was glad for Nick to have a peer he could confide in. Katie, on the other hand, had no close friends. When Kristy and Nick left, I went inside and knocked on her bedroom door.

"Yeah?" she answered.

"Got a minute? I'd like to talk," I said. She opened the door, then flopped onto her bed. I sat on the edge.

I suddenly realized I didn't know what to say. I wasn't even sure if it was my place to get involved in this matter between a daughter and her father. But it also wasn't right for a father to leave his kids without seeing both of them first. Katie looked at me with tearful eyes, then turned away. Had it been in my power, I would have stopped at nothing to ease the hurt in those eyes!

"You said you wanted to talk," she reminded me.

"I heard about your dad," I said.

She started to cry. "Please go."

"Katie, I...."

"Leave me alone!"

I should have gotten up and left, but I couldn't. In a few hours, her father would leave the state and it would be months, possibly years, before she would see him again. She deserved the opportunity to say good-bye to him face to face. How much more difficult would the separation be if she were denied that chance? "Look, I think you should see your father."

"If he doesn't want to see me, I don't want to see him!" She sprang from her bed and dashed out of the house. Through the window I watched as she stormed across the yard and started down the busy road we lived on.

Concerned for her safety, I ran after her. "Kate, get back in the house. Now!"

"You can't tell me what to do. You're not my father!"

At that moment, the irony struck me. A parent is virtually guaranteed a place in a child's heart regardless whether or not he deserves it. But no matter how much a stepparent loves a child, he must always earn his place in a child's heart, and then work to maintain it. Even then, it is the child's decision whether or not to accept the stepparent. I stopped running, and Katie stopped a few paces further. "You're right, I'm not your father, but I do care about you." Just then a string of cars whizzed past. "Katie, you need to go back to the house. *We* need to go back to the house. It's not safe out here."

She stomped back to her room and slammed the door behind her. I sought the couch in the living room. As important as I believed it was for her to see her father, I knew I couldn't force her. Feeling helpless and more lost than ever, I began flipping channels. How would I explain to Kristy what had happened? What should I have done differently? Had I overstepped my boundaries? Why had I gotten involved in the first place?

A little while later Katie came into the living room. "Hey," she said. I looked up. "I'm sorry."

"Me too," I said. The standoff was over.

When Kristy and I were dating, Katie would often ride with me when I ran errands, and sometimes I'd treat her to ice cream while we were out. "Why don't we go get some ice cream?" I said.

She nodded. We drove in silence until she said, "I wish my mommy and daddy would get back together. You could go back with your wife, and everything would be fine." This was the same girl

who had happily clicked pictures at our wedding a few weeks earlier,

and the same girl who had pretended not to notice when I had

slipped rocks and pinecones into her trick-or-treat bag as we

circulated her neighborhood during Halloween the year before. I had

no idea that she still harbored a hope that her parents would reunite.

Yet I could understand how to her, reconciling the two failed

marriages would yield a tidy resolution to the circumstances that

surrounded us. Of course, she could not yet fathom the complexities

of adult relationships or the variables that sometimes led to their

failures.

Then she blurted, "Rufus has to get his nuts cut off." Rufus

was their dog, which lived with their father. I was sure this bit of

information had come via Nick.

"How come?" I asked.

"Because in Florida he will have to stay in a kennel. It won't

hurt him, will it?"

Trying not to cringe I said, "No, I'm sure they'll numb him

up really well first. They might even give him some sleeping gas, so

he won't be awake for it."

"I hope so. I wish they didn't have to do that to him." It was her attempt to grasp something—anything—out of this whole mess that she could wrap her mind around. To her, Rufus's plight was the one thing that was certain, and she was clinging to it.

At the ice cream shop, we each ordered a soft-serve vanilla cone. We moved to the picnic table farthest away from the building and licked our ice cream in the quiet dusk. Nearby two stray kittens wrestled with each other in the shadows.

I finished my cone first. "I'm not trying to be pushy. I'm just making the offer. If you want to see your father, I'll take you there. If you don't, that's fine and we'll go home."

"Can I get him a card?"

"Of course, you can."

From the ice cream shop, we drove to the town pharmacy. I gave her a few dollars and waited in the car while she selected a card. This was a personal matter, one she needed to handle on her own. When she returned to the car, she signed the card and sealed it in the envelope.

A short while later we pulled up to her father's place and found him piling his belongings into the back of his pick-up truck.

Katie followed him inside. She stayed for just a few minutes before returning to the car. We drove home without a word.

As we walked across our driveway, she gave me a quick hug, then darted into the house.

I paused alone in the darkness to dry my eyes.

On A Rainy Day

The rain fell in torrents that morning, crashing against the
metal roof of Ed Hoff's mobile home with a relentless roar. Ed
spread two flimsy slats in the dusty Venetian blind that hung in the
kitchen window. His view was distorted by the thousands of
droplets that splattered and streaked the pane, but he could see that
the standing water had swallowed the curb at the far end of his street
near the front of the trailer park. It lapped at the bottom of the black
Chevy Cavalier parked there. "Marietta ain't gonna believe..." he
mumbled, then stopped. *Where did that come from?* he wondered.
Marietta wasn't coming home.

He tried to light a cigarette, but his butane lighter was empty.
He tossed it onto the worn, stained counter next to the stove.
Crouching in front of the stove, he turned on a front burner and lit
his cigarette in the pale blue flame. After two deep drags he stood
and poured a cup of coffee. He smoked, sipped his coffee, and
watched the rain. In time he poured a second cup, then a third, and
lit another cigarette.

He opened the refrigerator, removed the lid from a bowl of
leftover hamburger with macaroni, and sniffed it. It was still good.

He also took the remaining half of the Italian hoagie that had been

the previous night's dinner, then closed the door. Next, he took the

bag from Nickel's Pharmacy from the counter and up-ended it,

spilling out three packs of nicotine gum. He stuffed the hamburger

macaroni and hoagie half into the bag, then took two packs of Dorals

from the open carton atop the fridge and dropped them into the bag.

Marietta hated his smoking.

Ed moved to the living room and turned on the TV. The

meteorologist on WBOC in nearby Dover, Delaware said flood

warnings had been issued for all of Delaware and parts of Maryland,

Pennsylvania, and New Jersey, and that residents were advised not to

travel unless it was necessary. He also said some areas could see

more rain that day than they had since Hurricane Floyd had brushed

the central Atlantic Coast in 1999, five years earlier. A pang shot

through Ed's chest at the mention of that day. It was a day much

like this one. He turned off the TV. Soon it was time to leave for

work. He finished his coffee and extinguished his cigarette in the

already too-full ashtray on the coffee table.

Outside the rain roared. Ed paused in the front doorway for a

moment surveying the puddles surrounding his dilapidated Dodge

Shadow, a jalopy adorned with peeling maroon paint, rust splotches, and just two of its wheel covers. He dashed toward his car; thankful he hadn't locked it. The cold droplets stung his skin and soaked through his shirt. He placed his lunch on the passenger's side floor, started the engine, and turned the wipers to high. Back and forth they flung water from his view, leaving streaks in their swath with each pass. He pressed the lighter into its socket, waited, then lit a cigarette.

Ed pulled away from the curb and crept into the deep water at the front of the park as he made his way toward the main road. By now the water had reached the bottoms of the doors on the black Cavalier, the lone car at this end of the street. He didn't know if the car ran. He'd never seen it move, and thought it might have been stolen, joy-ridden, then abandoned where it sat for the police to one day find.

When he reached the entrance of the tiny community he came to a stop. Movement on the passenger's side floor caught his eye. It was water sloshing back and forth. "Damn!" he said as he grabbed his lunch bag and emptied it onto the seat. Fortunately, only his hoagie wrapping was wet, but not wet enough to ruin the sandwich. As for the water, he assumed it had entered through a rust hole beneath the carpet. It would drain through that same hole.

Route thirteen was nearly deserted. It occurred to Ed as he drove north through Smyrna toward Kent County Tire Center that the younger guys in the shop probably wouldn't show up for work. *Lazy damned kids!* he thought. *They'll use any excuse for a day off!* He knew that they often referred to him as Old Hermit when he was out of earshot, and they usually excluded him from their conversations. He cared little what they thought of him, and he ignored them when they bragged about how much beer they could drink or lied about the girls they'd had. *Too much nineteen-year-old drama for me!* He knew that in time, one by one these kids would leave to pursue other paths in life. As they left, new kids would take their places. It happened over and over. Only he had remained since the fledgling days of the store eighteen years ago, mounting tires day after day. He took pride in his tenure. His job suited him. Furthermore, nobody could say he was flighty.

The road sloped downward as he neared the Commerce Street intersection, and he slowed before reaching the pool that had collected there. As he crossed the intersection, he estimated the depth at nearly a foot. Just then a fast-moving blue Ford Expedition

hit the water from the opposite direction. A wave shot from its

wheels and gushed over Ed's windshield and roof. "Idiot!" he

shouted, but he knew the other driver wouldn't hear him.

Ed despised the SUV crowd. Most of these folks were

transplants from the north who were gobbling up the new houses and

townhomes that had been multiplying like cockroaches west of town.

To Ed it seemed that the majority of these people were uppity and

had no use for the locals. Like most locals, he had no use for them.

Still, he knew that Marietta had secretly wanted a townhouse

in one of the new communities. Although the thought of moving to

a townhouse and being surrounded by these out of town jerks made

him cringe, he would have honored Marietta's wish if she'd asked.

She was a good woman and he would have done anything to make

her happy if only she'd asked. But she never did.

He knew of the sorrow she harbored for her inability to

conceive, but he swore any inadequacy she felt as his wife was

unwarranted. Still, she rarely asked for anything. Instead, she

lavished him with love. He thought that maybe their situation had

brought them even closer.

When Ed arrived at work, he pulled into the gravel lot behind the building. The ditch separating the lot from the soybean field behind it flowed like a muddy river toward Duck Creek. The only other vehicle in the lot was the road service truck, which Dave, the owner, drove to and from work. *I knew the children wouldn't show up!*

Ed gathered the contents of his soggy bag and ran toward the back door of the building. Dave met him just inside the door. "What are you doing here?" Dave asked.

"What do you mean? It's almost time to open," Ed said.

"Not today. The governor's just declared a state of emergency. They don't want anybody out in this mess."

"Oh. I didn't hear. But don't we have to be open? What if one of the big rigs out on route one has a blow-out?"

Dave laughed. "Route one's closed. Flooded out. Thirteen's probably going to be closed soon. They say this storm is going to get a lot worse before it gets better. Only reason I'm here is because the water shorted the sensor on the warehouse door and the alarm was going off."

Ed shook his head and sighed. He groped his pocket for a cigarette, then remembered he didn't have a lighter. Dave didn't smoke, so there was no point in asking him.

"Don't worry. I'm still going to pay you guys for today. It's not your fault we can't be open."

"It's not that. It's just...." Ed's voice faltered. He looked toward the floor.

"I know," Dave said, patting Ed's shoulder, his tone suddenly soft. "Hey, take the day and watch TV or read a book or something. Try to occupy yourself however you can, and hope things are back to normal tomorrow."

Ed nodded. "Okay. See you then." He walked back to his car. There was no reason to run now, for he was already soaked. Besides, he would change as soon as he got home.

Once inside his car, he pushed in the lighter, placed the items from his lunch bag on the seat, and lit a cigarette. Then he started the engine and headed home.

When he reached the Commerce Street intersection the water was deeper than it had been before and a green Honda Civic sat moored in the north bound lanes like a buoy. By the rapid movement of twigs and other floating debris Ed knew the water was now moving with a swift current as it sought the lower lands east of town. As he started through, he had to fight the wheel to keep the car from being pushed to the left. The water was now up to his bumper, and soon it gushed under the doors, flooding the floor of the car. He could feel his tires fighting for grip as the floodwaters shoved his car from the right, much as he imagined they had had swept Marietta's red Hyundai Accent from the rickety wooden bridge over Duck Creek in the marsh land east of Smyrna five years earlier. He shuddered and pressed onward.

Once home, he slogged from his car to the front steps. He shivered as he stood on the tiny landing outside the front door fumbling with the key. As he swung the door open, he thought he caught a whiff of the hot chocolate Marietta used to make for him when he came home from work on those cold winter nights. He smiled and sniffed again, but the aroma was gone.

Marietta's not coming home. Ever. Although he had known this to be true, until that moment it had never seemed so real—so *final.* He now realized that a part of him had harbored a hope that one day she would return. Irrational as he knew that was, there was that small part of him that had refused to let go. But now, as he stood hunched and shivering before his open door, that hope flickered and died as if extinguished by the stinging droplets. It succumbed to the cold rain just as Marietta had five years prior. For the first time ever, Ed felt the hollowness of being all alone. "No. No!" he shouted as he dashed into the trailer and thrust the door closed.

He turned on the TV. WBOC had suspended its normal programming to provide non-stop coverage of the storm. He glanced at the weather map on the screen, only half interested as he passed through the living room and into the kitchen. He lit a cigarette from the stove. Marietta hated his smoking. She loved candles. Ed took several quick puffs, then extinguished his butt beneath the kitchen faucet. He then went to the bedroom, shed his sopping clothes, and donned a robe. He took the candle she kept atop her night stand. Returning to the kitchen, he lit it from the stove, then shielded the flame as he carried it to the living room. He placed it atop the TV.

Next, he went back to the kitchen, tore open a pack of nicotine gum, and shoved three pieces into his mouth. He raised the top of the stove, blew out the pilot light, and then cranked all of the burners to high. As he chewed his gum he settled onto the sofa and closed his eyes while the television blathered on about the storm.

He would see Marietta soon.

I Was My Brother's Witness

It was a Friday afternoon and school was finally done. I shoved my books into my locker, then hurried to meet my brother Todd at his locker. Since we'd moved, he and I always walked to and from school together.

You see, when our family lived in New Jersey, Todd and I went to different schools and we rode different busses. But our dad got laid off from his job at Lucid Chemicals, and after that our mom went to live with her sister, Aunt Beth, for what must have been the umpteenth time. This time she said it was for good. After she left Dad realized he couldn't make ends meet, so he moved us in with our grandparents in Oxford, Pennsylvania. It was a small town. Dad called it Bumfuck, but I figured it would do until he found a job, Mom came back, and we could get a place of our own and be a family again. I'm older now, so I know now just how naive that sounds, but at the time that's what I believed.

Todd was a year older than I was, but we looked so much alike people often thought we were twins. I was in seventh grade and Todd was in eighth, so we both went to Oxford Middle School. The kids called it Ox Fart Middle, and it was close enough to Nana and Pop-pop's that we had to walk. I knew Todd was unhappy there. He was shy and had a hard time making friends. When we were alone that's all he ever talked about—wishing he had friends, wishing he could fit in, wishing we could move back to New Jersey where he had friends.

As usual, the hallway was crowded, and the traffic moved slowly. When I got to Todd's locker his back was toward me as he talked with two other kids in his class, Mike Walker and Billy Rudd. I knew Mike because he delivered the morning paper to our house every day, and he came around collecting money every two weeks. Billy hung around Mike almost all the time. He thought he was cool, but he pretty much did whatever Mike said.

"You're not gonna wimp out on us, are you, Jersey boy?" Mike said to Todd with a sly smile.

"No. I'm gonna do it. I really am," Todd said.

"Do what?" I asked. Billy sneered at me.

"Nothin'. You've gotta walk home by yourself today. I got something to do," Todd said to me without turning around.

"What are you doing?" I asked.

"I told you. Nothin'! Now get out of here, will you?"

"But...."

"Go on, dumbass! Get outta here!"

"Asshole!" I said almost under my breath as I turned away. I was sure Todd heard me, and I wanted him to, but he didn't come after me. I almost wished he had, but he was too busy trying to get in good with these guys.

The truth is, Todd *was* an asshole, but he'd only gotten that way recently. Until last month he was usually a decent kid. He was okay all summer, even after we moved to Oxford, until right after school started. But since then he'd been treating me like crap and putting me down in front of other kids. I'd always looked up to him and tried my best to be like him, but suddenly it was like I didn't know who he was anymore. I didn't know why he'd changed, and I even wondered if I'd done something to cause it. Whatever the case, I wished I could find a way to make him respect me so maybe he would treat me better.

Still, Todd and the other two were up to something, and I was dying to know what. I walked down the hall, blending in with the other students, then ducked into the first classroom I came to. From the doorway I watched them. Todd closed his locker and they headed my way. I waited until they passed, then followed them, taking care to maintain a safe distance. The talking, shouting, and laughing of the other kids drowned out any conversation I might have overheard between the trio ahead of me.

I lost sight of them when they reached the double doors at the front of the building and were swept outside by the current of the crowd. Once I passed through the doors, I spotted them. They had broken away from the crowd and were running toward the woods beside the school. Seconds later they disappeared into the thick foliage. I just *had* to find out what they were up to.

Moving with the crowd, I continued toward the parking lot where a row of busses awaited those fortunate enough to live a distance from the school. Then I turned and headed down the sidewalk as if I was going home. I had to be careful. Todd and the others might have been watching me.

After walking several yards along the sidewalk, I veered toward the woods and dashed to where I'd seen them enter. There I found a path. I paused. In the distance I heard their voices; they were already deep in the woods. I crept along the path using caution not to step on twigs or rustle the new-fallen leaves any more than I had to. Finally, I came upon them. They were standing in a clearing, not making a sound, listening. I ducked behind a thicket of briars.

"I'm telling you Billy, it's nothing. There's nobody there. You're freakin' paranoid, man," Mike said.

"I coulda sworn I heard something. Ah, maybe you're right," Billy said.

Mike took a pack of Marlboros from his jacket pocket,

flipped open the top, and took a cigarette. He motioned for Billy to

take one. Billy did. Mike then held the pack toward Todd. "Here.

Have a smoke." Todd hesitated, then reached for a cigarette. He

fumbled with it between his fingers. Next Mike pulled a lighter

from his pocket. He lit his own cigarette, then Billy's, then Todd's.

After Mike's final drag, he dropped his butt on the ground

Mike and Billy each took a deep drag. Mike tilted his head

back and exhaled his lungful of smoke in an upward column while

Billy blew smoke rings. Todd sucked at his cigarette, inhaled, and

choked. Billy laughed. "Pansy ass," he said.

"It'll get easier with practice," Mike said. They continued to

smoke, Mike and Billy enjoying their cigarettes, Todd suffering

through his.

After Mike's final drag, he dropped his butt on the ground

and squashed it with his toe. "Okay, like we said, if you want to

hang out with us, you hafta prove you're worth our time. Here's the

plan. You know old lady Berkheimer, right? Teaches English,

classroom's on the back side of the school, second floor. Know how

she's got all those flower pots with spider plants and shit hanging in

her windows? Well, you're gonna take some rocks and throw them

through her windows and knock down her plants. If you take out

just one of her plants, you're in. If you don't, you lose. Simple as

that. Got it?"

Todd nodded. His face had lost its color and looked like the white of a hard-boiled egg. I knew he was scared.

From the clearing there were paths leading in three other directions. I watched to see which path they took, then waited until they were out of sight before following. I didn't go far before I saw them again. Near the edge of the woods they were kicking through the leaves searching for suitable rocks. I watched from behind a tree with a trunk barely wide enough to conceal my body.

After a few minutes Mike said, "Six rocks. That should be enough."

"Yeah, if you can't do it in six tries, you got a girl's arm!" Billy said.

Todd took the rocks and headed out of the woods and across the back lawn of the school. Mike and Billy followed, but stopped a short distance beyond the edge of the woods. I crept to the edge of the woods and watched as Todd dropped all but one of the rocks at his feet. He hurled the first rock, then picked up the second and cocked his arm back just as the first one crashed through a window inches to the left of one of Mrs. Berkheimer's flower pots. Todd's second throw went high, his third low.

Then one of the rear doors of the school opened. "Shit!" Mike said as he and Billy dashed toward the woods and me. I raced down the path and crouched behind the tree where I'd hidden

minutes earlier. I was sure they would see me, but they didn't look

my way as they flew past.

"Hey, get back here you little son of a bitch!" a man's voice

bellowed. Then Todd ran past, followed several seconds later by

Crazy Walt, one of the school janitors. Walt stopped next to the tree

where I hid and stood panting, gasping for breath. On a typical day

old Walt was a big man, but on this day he seemed like a giant as he

towered over me. By accident our eyes met. In one swift move he

snatched my jacket collar and jerked me to my feet. "So, there you

are, you little bastard! You're gonna pay for this if I have to take it

out of your hide!"

So that was it! Crazy Walt had confused me with Todd, and

he thought I was the one who had thrown the rocks through the

window. I opened my mouth to tell him it wasn't me, but I couldn't

speak. Later I thought this was probably a good thing. If Crazy

Walt really was as crazy as the other kids said, had I crossed him at

that moment he would have probably strangled me on the spot.

Then he would have disposed of my body by whatever means crazy

janitors used to dispose of troublesome students' bodies.

Gripping my shoulder so tightly my arm went numb, Crazy

Walt marched me to see Mr. Benson, the school principal. Behind the closed heavy wooden door of Mr. Benson's office Walt gave him his take on what had just happened. I sat on the hard-wooden bench outside the door where Walt had deposited me. I felt like I would be sick.

When the door opened, Walt glared at me as he passed. Then Mr. Benson stepped from his office. "Mr. Quinland, I understand you're responsible for some rather serious damage to school property. Have a seat in my office while I inspect the damage and notify the authorities."

Mr. Benson's office was a tiny room crowded by just a few pieces of furniture. I didn't see how he could meet comfortably with students' parents in there. I took one of the cushionless chairs facing Mr. Benson's desk. It felt much like the hard-wooden bench outside his door. The white-faced wall clock overhead showed three o'clock exactly. *I should be home by now,* I thought. *Todd's probably watching cartoons or playing video games while I'm stuck here, accused of what he did!* It wasn't fair. I wanted Mr. Benson to come back so I could explain what really happened. Crazy Walt had made a big mistake! How could he confuse me with Todd anyway? Todd wore a brown jacket. Mine was blue!

The red second hand moved at its slow, steady pace; a pace unaffected by my wish for it to speed up. It rounded all twelve numbers on the clock face, completing its circuit without feeling and with unvarying speed, only to make another trip around the face. The clock was painful to watch! *How long will I have to sit here and wait?*

Mr. Benson's chair was a cushy stuffed leather high back, no doubt the most comfortable chair in the school. I tried to imagine what it would be like to come to school every morning and sink into that soft leather. Atop the cabinet beside his desk sat a framed family portrait including his wife, two daughters, and a shaggy white dog. Mr. Benson's older daughter was pretty. She looked about seventeen. I guessed the younger one to be about fourteen, two years older than I was, and she was really cute. If I'd guessed her age right, she would be a freshman in high school, and undoubtedly more worldly than I. I tried to imagine what it would be like to hold her hand and then to kiss her. Thinking of her I almost forgot my plight.

Mr. Benson's door burst open. My fantasy was shattered, much like Mrs. Berkheimer's window.

Mr. Benson entered his office followed by a uniformed police officer. Mr. Benson sank into his cushy chair but held a stiff posture as his eyes burned into mine. The policeman stood uncomfortably in the tiny space just inside the door, his holstered gun pointing at the floor. In his left hand he held a note pad and, in his right, a pen. "Mr. Quinland, I'm Corporal Westerly with the Oxford Borough Police. I'm sure you know why I'm here, but I'd like to hear your side." His firearm jiggled as he spoke.

I swallowed. It wasn't a real swallow, but a shallow one I didn't know was coming and couldn't have stopped if I'd wanted to. It was then I realized how dry my mouth was and how sticky my tongue had become. But this was my chance to tell what had really happened. I was innocent! I didn't do it! I was nothing more than an onlooker, a bystander who through plain bad luck happened to be in the wrong place at the wrong time. I didn't do it!

But I knew who did.

Dare I rat out my brother? Sure, he was the one who had broken the window, but he was also my older brother. He would beat me up if I told, but that didn't worry me. It wasn't like the asshole had never done that before. But asshole or not, he was still something of a hero to me. Through the years, when it really mattered, he had looked out for me. All those times when Mom left, Todd cooked me dinner and even helped me with my homework while Dad was at work. When Tom Griffin, the neighborhood bully at our old house in New Jersey, had picked on me, Todd threatened to beat his head in with a baseball bat. And when we started at our new school in Oxford, Todd had walked me to and from school every day until now, even though I knew he didn't want to. Could I roll over on someone who once took care of me, who I looked up to, and wanted to be like? No, I couldn't rat him out.

But what about Mike and Billy? They were the ones who'd put Todd up to it, all so he could hang out with them. If it weren't for them, none of this would have happened. They deserved to be ratted out! But if I ratted them out, I was sure they would drag Todd into it anyway, and then I'd have Mike and Billy out to kill me, and probably Todd, too. *Better not mention any names,* I thought.

"Mr. Quinland?" Corporal Westerly said.

"I was leaving school when I saw these three kids running into the woods. I was curious, so I followed them."

Corporal Westerly scribbled something on his note pad. "Describe these kids."

No details! I thought. "They were ordinary looking kids. You know, just normal kids."

"Boys? Girls?"

"Boys."

"How tall?"

I thought for a minute. "They were average."

"Hair color?"

"Two were blonde, and one had dark hair." These were lies. Only Todd was of average height and had blonde hair, like me. Mike and Billy were both taller and had dark hair.

More scribbling on the note pad. "Okay, then what?"

"I was curious where they were going. I'm new here, and I thought maybe they had a fort or something back in the woods I didn't know about. So, I followed them."

More scribbling. "Okay...."

I decided to leave out the part about the cigarettes. It didn't matter anyway. "They went down one path, then took another one that came out at the back of the school. At first, I stayed back and hid behind a tree so they wouldn't know I was following them, but when they went out of the woods, I moved up so I could see what was happening."

Corporal Westerly made even more notes this time. "Then what happened?"

"All three of them left the woods, but two stayed back near the woods. Only one kid went up to the school and threw the rocks. But then the back door opened and Crazy Wa... uh, I mean the janitor came out and started yelling and chasing him."

"That would be our custodian, Mr. Walter Houlahan," Mr. Benson said.

"Then what?" Corporal Westerly asked while still making notes.

"The two kids closest to the woods ran toward me. I ran back to the tree where I was hiding before and got behind it. Those two kids ran past me first, then the kid who threw the rocks ran by. Mr. Houlahan chased them into the woods but stopped next to the tree I was hiding behind. He saw me, and he thought I was the one who threw the rocks."

Corporal Westerly finished his notes, then asked, "Is this the best description you can give me of the other three kids?" I nodded. Corporal Westerly rubbed his chin. "Well, I've got to say, this doesn't look good." My stomach flipped. "Mr. Houlahan says it was you and you alone, and he says he chased you and caught you seconds later and only about seventy yards from where the incident occurred. You say it wasn't you, and that there were *three* other kids involved, but you can't give me detailed descriptions of any of them. Can you see why I'm having a problem with this?"

I nodded and bowed my head. It was no use. Even if I ratted out all three of them, I doubted Corporal Westerly or Mr. Benson would have believed me. I dreaded whatever punishment awaited me here at school as well as at Nana and Pop-pop's. Dad would probably ground me, but even worse, I wondered if he would ever trust me again. It infuriated me to think that this was all over something I didn't even do. Todd wouldn't be the source of his disappointment, I would be, and all for something he did!

Mr. Benson's phone rang. "Hello.... Thanks. We'll be right out." He stood, then said to Corporal Westerly, "The boy's father is here."

"Oh man, I am so dead!" I muttered once they had left the room. My stomach felt as if I'd gobbled a pail of uncured concrete, and the tears that streamed from my eyes did nothing to cool my burning cheeks. *I didn't do it! It's not fair!*

The second hand on the wall clock now seemed to move slower than before. I longed for this moment to be over, but the second hand crept from one number to the next at such an agonizing pace I couldn't watch. I could hear Mr. Benson, Corporal Westerly, and my father talking just beyond Mr. Benson's office door, but I couldn't hear what they were saying. Finally, I looked at the photo of Mr. Benson's family and tried to concentrate on his daughter once more, but my fantasy would not return. My eyes were drawn back to the clock. The seconds ticked by, then a minute, then two. I looked away.

Mr. Benson's cushy chair had twelve large brown buttons sewn into the seat back cushion. There were six pencils and two pens in the pencil holder next to the computer monitor atop his desk. There were fourteen manila folders in a neat stack next to his family's photo, and there were 128 little squares in the grid that shielded the fluorescent light overhead. I counted all of these things in the twenty-three minutes I waited alone in Mr. Benson's office.

When the door opened, it startled me. Mr. Benson came in first, followed by my father, who closed the door. Corporal Westerly had apparently left. I should have recognized this as a good sign, but it worried me instead. Corporal Westerly had seemed like the person who least wanted to kill me. That included my father, judging by the look on his face. Mr. Benson sat in his cushy chair while my father stood awkwardly in the spot where Corporal Westerly had been.

"Mr. Quinland, you are in a lot of trouble. Your actions this afternoon show a complete lack of respect for school property and the faculty, not to mention your own father. Furthermore, you have demonstrated a serious lapse in good judgement. Normally, in a case such as this, the police would have taken you to Juvenile Hall where you would be brought up on criminal charges." If he was trying to scare me, he was doing a good job. "That's exactly what would have happened to you if your father hadn't intervened. You owe him a huge debt of gratitude. He has agreed to pay for the damages, and in exchange, the school will not prosecute you.

"There won't be any criminal charges pressed, but you're far from off the hook, young man. I'm giving you a three-day suspension, which will remain on your school record permanently, and I trust that your father will make you pay him back in one way or another for what you've cost him." Mr. Benson glanced at my father, who nodded. "Today is Friday. Your suspension will begin Monday. I expect you back in school next Thursday, but not before then. Have I made myself clear?"

I had been staring at the front of Mr. Benson's desk. I nodded without looking up.

"Then you may leave," Mr. Benson said.

My father and I walked to the car in silence, although I had to half-trot to keep up with his long, angry strides. As we drove out of the parking lot Dad said, "I don't believe this! First, your brother comes home reeking of cigarettes, and now you're destroying school property! What the hell's wrong with you two?"

Todd got caught smoking? Good! He's not getting off totally free after all!

When we got home, Dad sat Todd and me down on the sofa in the living room. "I don't know what's gotten into you two. You for smoking," he said to Todd, "and you for throwing rocks at the school windows," he said to me. Todd's eyes grew wide and his mouth fell open as he looked at me. It was obvious this was the first he'd heard. His face then became Marlboro red. Either Dad didn't notice, or he must have figured Todd's red face was caused by his shame for smoking.

Dad gave us quite a bitching out, and he went full circle from "What the hell's the matter with you two?" to "Your mother's to blame for all of this!" to "I know the move has been tough on you, but it's temporary, I promise," and finally to "Look, we can't undo what's been done, but we can avoid repeating our mistakes." Then came the punishment phase of his lecture. "I think you both need time to think about what you've done. You're grounded for two weeks. During that time, you are to scrape the loose paint off every inch of the outside of this house so your grandfather and I can get a coat of paint on it before winter sets in. After that, there'll be plenty of leaves to rake. You'll also help him trim the shrubs and do whatever odd jobs he asks. And on rainy days, you are to clean the basement. That means every day after school, Saturdays and Sundays, too. Got it?" Todd and I nodded. "Good. Now go to your room."

Todd and I shared a room down the hall from Nana and Pop-pop's and across from Dad's. When we were both in the room Todd shut the door. "You threw rocks at the school windows?" he asked innocently.

"No, asshole, you did!" I said. "I know because I followed you. I was hiding in the woods, and I saw the whole thing. Crazy Walt chased you into the woods, and you ran right past me. But he found me and thought I was you!"

Todd sat on his bed. His gaze fell to the floor. "Gonna tell?"

"I don't know," I said. I was being honest. Although I was sure Mr. Benson and Corporal Westerly wouldn't have believed me, I thought our father might. At least I wouldn't be grounded then. Besides, Todd really was an asshole. But no matter what I decided, it was clear I had the upper hand with Todd, at least for the moment. I thought to ask him why he had done it, but I already knew. I had nothing to gain by making him explain.

The next two weeks went by more quickly than I'd expected. Even though we were being punished, I was surprised to find that I enjoyed the time I spent working with Todd, and I really think he enjoyed spending time with me. Things between us were a lot like they used to be, only better. I didn't rat him out, and suddenly it seemed that he regarded me in a special way, almost like an equal. I thought maybe I'd finally earned his respect after all.

When I returned to school after my suspension, I didn't know what to expect. I thought maybe I'd be shunned by students and teachers alike, but that wasn't the case. Of course, Mrs. Berkheimer's window had been replaced by then. Although she didn't have much to say to me, the other teachers acted like nothing had happened. Among the kids it was different, though. I soon learned I was the talk of the student body. Some feared me, some revered me, but everybody knew who I was. Overnight I had become popular!

Mike and Billy rejected Todd, for he had failed to knock down any of Mrs. Berkheimer's flower pots. Instead, they teased him, saying he threw like a little girl. I'm sure they also razzed him for letting me take the fall for him, but they kept their secret to themselves.

Things had turned out okay, and I probably should have been content to let the whole incident blow over, but something still nagged me. I had been punished for an act I didn't commit. Furthermore, among my peers I had received wrongful recognition, both good and bad, for that act. I felt like a phony! There was only one way I knew to fix this.

My restriction at home ended on the Saturday morning two weeks after the whole thing began. That day I got up early, left the house unnoticed, and hurried to the school. I was sure nobody else would be there. I walked along the edge of the woods as I made my way to the rear of the building and gathered a few decent sized rocks along the way. When I reached the back side of the school, I sought Mrs. Berkheimer's classroom, then positioned myself on the lawn just as Todd had. I clutched one of the rocks, then focused on the large clay pot which hung in the center window behind the new pane of glass. I cocked my arm back, then hurled the rock.

Its trajectory was perfect, and the rock found its target. Glass shards, pottery fragments, clumps of dirt, and a surprised spider plant all fell to Mrs. Berkheimer's floor.

Just then a hand clasped my shoulder from behind. *Shit!* I just knew it was Crazy Walt. With only the two of us there at the school I didn't want to think about what he'd do to me. Slowly I turned my to face him.

But it wasn't Crazy Walt. It was Mike Walker, and he was grinning at me. He dropped his empty newspaper sack and reached for his pocket. "Nice throw, kid! Here. Have a smoke."

The Hunter and The Hunted

It was a frantic day. Winter lay ahead. She had so much to do—a home to prepare, food reserves to secure, young ones to tend to…. She scurried on her way, ever conscious of the tasks she must fulfill, of the waning season, of the waning day. She scurried, alert to the ever-present possibility of danger ahead.

Her rapid movement caught his attention. With eyes trained on her, his muscles tensed. As she neared, he took a breath and braced himself, poised for action.

At once she spotted him. Their eyes connected, hers round and startled, his piercing and fiery. She turned away. Maybe he hadn't really seen her. But she knew he had. And she knew she was well within his striking range. He was faster and more powerful than she. Furthermore, he could utter one call and many more of his kind would join him.

Should she halt? Perhaps in the absence of a challenge he would become disinterested, thus sparing her a horrible fate. Maybe she could outwit him, though his kind seldom fell for trickery. Should she flee? The possibility of eluding her pursuer was narrow;

he would certainly be agitated when he fell her. But there was that chance; if she were lucky, her escape would be a clean one.

Her gut said, *"Run!"*

She darted past his vantage point without slowing. A flash of red, a wail—a cry of battle as he swooped behind her, larger and more mighty than she had imagined. Foreboding welled in her gut. She was at once tiny and weak.

The battle was lost before it began.

She stopped. He slowed as he neared her. She cowered. He approached her with cautious, yet deliberate strides, sizing her up, ever conscious of the trickery her kind was known to impart. He snorted, then growled, "License and registration, please."

The Shopping Cart

"Now, just where in the hell did we park the car?" the old man asked without looking up from his shopping cart. He leaned on it as he pushed it along.

"It's this way," his daughter replied as she stepped ahead, making sure it was safe for him to cross the thoroughfare separating the curb in front of Zingo's Grocery Mart from the rows of parked cars beyond.

He glanced at her as a puff of autumn air blew her dark hair about her neck on this chilly overcast day. For the first time he noticed how gray she had become. It must've happened overnight, he thought. Still, there was a familiar beauty about her. Damned if she doesn't look like Doris! He winced. Although Doris had passed away three years prior, there were still moments—painful moments such as this—when he had to remind himself that she was gone.

"Debra, are we going the right way? I don't remember parking this far away."

"Dad, I can see the car from here. Are you sure you don't want me to push the cart?"

"No! I told you, I've got the god-damned cart! The day I can no longer push a shopping cart is the day you can tell Father O'Harra to give me my last rights! No decent able-bodied man would let a woman push a cart while walking along beside her empty-handed."

"Have it your way," Debra mumbled.

"Speak up! What did you say?"

"Nothing."

He knew her divorce had been hard on her. Twenty-six years down the drain. He hated to think she had been to blame, but really, what had she done to prevent it? Tom was a winner, and the old man had seen it from the start. A football player and a member of the debate team in college, Tom knew how to talk to people—how to persuade them—and he knew how to get things done. He was smart, good-looking, and he had charm. When Debra had brought him home for the first time, he had thought to bring flowers for Doris. Furthermore, he had given a firm handshake and made eye contact when he spoke. A man's man if there ever was one. As the years ticked by, Tom had kept himself in shape. He worked hard, put in long hours, and traveled frequently. Over that time, he had engaged in numerous business ventures that others with less vision and drive had passed up. However, bad luck, bad timing, and unreliable partners had thwarted him. Why couldn't he get a break? Why couldn't he find associates with work ethics like his?

After Nate was born, Debra had focused all of her attention on him, not Tom. She hadn't lost the baby weight. To the contrary, she had added to it, and rarely did she do her hair or make-up. Furthermore, as time went by, she complained more and more that Tom was never around, but how could he be? He was a go-getter who was trying to provide the best for Nate and her. Why couldn't she see that? Nate had gone to college a thousand miles away in St. Louis, and he had accepted a job offer in the area after his graduation last year. But even in his absence Debra hadn't changed. With an attitude like hers, how could she have expected to hold onto a guy like Tom? Was it any wonder that he had sought younger, more vibrant women? Of course, it had come as a shock to learn of Tom's affairs, but hadn't Debra, in no small part, fueled his infidelity?

It wasn't until he had nearly rammed her with the cart that the old man realized she had stopped near the cart return. Staring into the distance, she was too preoccupied to notice how close he had come to bumping her. And then he saw it too. Parked downhill

across the aisle sat a maroon early model Dodge Challenger. "He

still has it…." Her voice trailed away.

Damn it! There was no mistaking it for anybody's other than

Fred Larson's car. It had been years—decades—since it had been a

regular fixture in front of their house, but now he scowled, repulsed

as if no time had passed at all. "Debra, don't you start!"

She blinked and turned away. "Things could have been so

different."

"That was a long time ago. I told you then, it's better this

way." To think, a grown woman getting caught up in her silly

teenage dreams! Even as a teen, she had been so starry-eyed, so

naïve! What the hell had she seen in Fred? His only ambition in life

was to be a car mechanic—a greasy god-damned mechanic! Sure,

he might have loved Debra and she certainly claimed to love him,

but they were kids! What did they know about love? And even if

things had worked out between them, just how did Fred ever expect

to afford a home and provide a stable future on a mechanic's salary?

How could I have let their relationship go on? Debra could do far

better than Fred, and Tom had been proof of that.

They continued to the car in silence. While loading their bags into the trunk Debra said, "I hear he runs the automotive program at Kent County Community College. He started teaching there in the evenings while he and his wife ran their auto repair shop during the day. When she got sick, they sold the business. She died of cancer a few years ago, but by then their kids were grown. He probably has grandkids now."

Clench-jawed, the old man said nothing. When the last of the bags had been loaded, he rolled the empty cart toward the cart return. He glared at Fred's Challenger again. Even in the gloomy light of this dreary day, its glossy paint and chrome wheels glistened. Clearly, these days it served him as a pampered fair-weather cruiser. Then he spotted a well-manicured man about Debra's age with a familiar gait moving toward the Challenger. He held the hand of a preschool aged boy, and the two chatted and laughed as they walked. Instead of continuing to the cart return, the old man aimed the cart toward Fred's car. Mustering the strength of a man twenty years his junior, he thrust it down the hill.

Other titles from Higher Ground Books & Media:

Wise Up to Rise Up by Rebecca Benston

A Path to Shalom by Steen Burke

Overcomer by Forrest Henslee

Breaking the Cycle by Willie Deeanjlo White

32 Days with Christ's Passion by Mark Etter

Knowing Affliction and Doing Recovery by John Baldasare

Out of Darkness by Stephen Bowman

I Don't Want to Be Like You by Maryanne Christiano-Mistretta

Anomaly by Derra Nicole Sabo

Ironies, Coincidences, & Absurdities by Henryk Hoffmann

Add these titles to your collection today!

http://highergroundbooksandmedia.com